The Frog Prince

First published in 2005 by
Franklin Watts
96 Leonard Street
London
EC2A 4XD

Franklin Watts Australia
Level 17/207 Kent Street
Sydney
NSW 2000

A CIP catalogue record for this book is available
from the British Library.

ISBN 0 7496 6156 9 (hbk)
ISBN 0 7496 6168 2 (pbk)

Series Editor: Jackie Hamley
Series Advisor: Dr Barrie Wade
Series Designer: Peter Scoulding

Printed in China

For Ginni, who likes woods and wells – H.R.

To Molly and Zachary, my budding
little artists – J.A. (Mummy)

The Frog Prince

Retold by Hilary Robinson

Illustrated by Jane Abbott

W
FRANKLIN WATTS
LONDON•SYDNEY

Long ago, in a castle
by a wood, lived a
beautiful Princess.

Deep in the wood was
a wishing well.

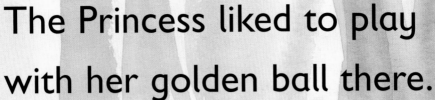

The Princess liked to play
with her golden ball there.

One day, she threw her
golden ball too high ...

... and it fell into the well.

The Princess cried and
cried. Then she heard
a little voice.

"Don't cry," croaked a frog.
"I will find your ball if you
promise to be my friend."

"I promise to be your
friend always if you find
my ball!" said the Princess.

The frog jumped into the
well and found the
Princess's golden ball.

But when he gave it to the Princess, she ran back to the castle.

The next day, there was a
knock at the castle door.

"Princess, Princess, please let me in," croaked a voice.

When the Princess saw the frog, she slammed the door.

"Who was that?"
asked the King.
"An ugly frog," replied
the Princess.

"I promised I'd always be his friend if he found my golden ball for me."

"Well, if he found your ball, then you must keep your promise," said the King.

So the frog came in and
sat beside the Princess.

At dinner, the frog ate
from the Princess's plate.

That night, he jumped onto
her bed to sleep beside her.

"Go away!" she cried.
But as she pushed the frog
away, he turned into a ...

... handsome Prince!
The Prince told her that a
witch had turned him into
a frog and made him live
in the well.

Only the touch of a
Princess's hand could
break the spell.

The Prince and Princess
soon fell in love.

And they lived happily
ever after.

Leapfrog has been specially designed to fit the requirements of the National Literacy Strategy. It offers real books for beginning readers by top authors and illustrators.

There are 37 Leapfrog stories to choose from:

* hardback